EDGE BOOKS

VAMPIRES

Real-Life Vampires

by Megan Kopp

Consultant: Bernd Heinrich
Emeritus Professor of Biology
University of Vermont
Burlington, Vermont

CAPSTONE PRESS
a capstone imprint

Property of Sequoyah
Regional Library System
www.sequoyahregionallibrary.org

Edge Books are published by Capstone Press,
151 Good Counsel Drive, P.O. Box 669, Mankato, Minnesota 56002.
www.capstonepub.com

Copyright © 2011 by Capstone Press, a Capstone imprint.
All rights reserved.
No part of this publication may be reproduced in whole or in part,
or stored in a retrieval system, or transmitted in any form or by any means,
electronic, mechanical, photocopying, recording, or otherwise, without
written permission of the publisher.
For information regarding permission, write to Capstone Press,
151 Good Counsel Drive, P.O. Box 669, Dept. R, Mankato, Minnesota 56002.
Printed in the United States of America in North Mankato, Minnesota.
032010
005740CGF10

Books published by Capstone Press are manufactured with paper
containing at least 10 percent post-consumer waste.

Library of Congress Cataloging-in-Publication Data
Kopp, Megan.
 Real-life vampires / by Megan Kopp.
 p. cm.—(Edge books. Vampires)
 Summary: "Describes some of nature's vampires, including vampire bats, leeches, lampreys, and mosquitoes"—Provided by publisher.
 Includes bibliographical references and index.
 ISBN 978-1-4296-4578-2 (library binding)
 1. Vampire bats—Juvenile literature. 2. Bloodsucking animals—Juvenile literature. I. Title. II. Series.
 QL737.C52K67 2011
 591.5'3—dc22   2010001691

Editorial Credits
Megan Peterson, editor; Veronica Correia, designer; Marcie Spence,
 media researcher; Laura Manthe, production specialist

Photo Credits
Adrian Warren/Ardea, 11
Apic/Getty Images, Inc., 7
Barry Mansell/Nature Picture Library, cover, 9 (bottom)
Bibliotheque Nationale, Paris, France/Archives Charret/The Bridgeman Art
 Library International, 19
Bill Beatty/Visuals Unlimited, 23
D. Parer & E. Parer-Cook/Ardea, 15
Dr. Merlin D. Tuttle/Bat Conservation International/Photo Researchers, Inc.,
 9 (top)
Fortean Picture Library, 5, 29
iStockphoto/ annedehaas, 17 (top); casdvm, 21; Dervical, 13; milehightraveler,
 20 (left); PEDRE, 17 (bottom); Sergey Lukianov, 18
Newscom, 24
NHPA/Photoshop, 16
Shutterstock/Dariusz Mijgier, 20 (right); djgis, 22 (top), 25 (mosquito); Dmitrijs
 Bindemanis, 22 (bottom); SasPartout, 25 (tick); Tom Grundy, 28
Underwood & Underwood/Corbis, 27

TABLE OF CONTENTS

In Search of a Vampire 4
I Want Your Blood 8
Beyond Batty 14
A Natural Truth 26

Glossary 30
Read More 31
Internet Sites 31
Index 32

Chapter 1

In Search of a Vampire

The moon is bright in the inky black sky. A dark figure flaps its wings, searching for food.

Suddenly the creature swoops down and lands on the ground. It slowly moves toward its snoozing **prey**. In a flash, the creature bites into its victim's flesh and drinks its blood.

If you think this creature sounds like the legendary Count Dracula, think again. It's the vampire bat from South America, one of nature's many vampires.

prey—an animal hunted by another animal for food

A Scary History

For thousands of years, people have feared vampires. They believed dead bodies rose from their graves to suck the blood of the living. In the 1600s and 1700s, the belief in vampires was widespread in eastern and central Europe. If someone died from an unknown illness, the person's family often blamed the death on a vampire attack.

First published in 1897, the novel *Dracula* kicked off the popular image of the wealthy and powerful vampire. But what made Count Dracula the prince of vampires? Behind the sickly pale face and thin body, the count had the strength of 20 men. He could change from human to bat and back again in the blink of an eye. Victims never saw Dracula approach them. Why? Because he had no shadow. Even Dracula's gaze had a deadly power. He used his eyes to put victims in a trance.

Today we know these scary vampire legends and stories are simply not true. But many vampire traits can be found in nature's beasts. From bats to bugs, bloodsuckers really do live in our world. And the truth of their bloodsucking ways can be scarier than any imaginary tale.

The Real Dracula

More than 500 years ago, terror swept through the kingdom of Wallachia in modern-day Romania. Prince Vlad Tepes ruled the land with an often bloody hand. He tortured his enemies by driving wooden stakes into their bodies. Prince Vlad, the son of Vlad Dracul, took the nickname "Dracula."

While researching vampires, author Bram Stoker came upon the name "Dracula." It was this scary name, along with European vampire legends, that helped Stoker write Dracula.

FACT: Dracula means "son of the dragon."

Vlad Dracula

Chapter 2

I Want Your Blood

Like the vampires of legend, vampire bats need blood to survive. But they don't actually suck blood—they lick it with their tongues. So what's the truth behind these real-life vampires?

Basic Bat Facts

Three types of vampire bats fly through the forests of Central and South America. The common vampire bat is the largest. These bats have a wingspan of 8 inches (20 centimeters). Their fur color ranges from gray to brown.

Like all bats, vampire bats are **nocturnal**. But unlike other bats, vampire bats don't land on their victims. Instead, they sneak up on their prey from the ground. Running and hopping, vampire bats approach their snoozing victims.

nocturnal—active at night

FACT: Female vampire bats spit up their blood meal and share it with those that can't find food.

Feed Me

Adult vampire bats live on blood alone. Baby vampire bats need their mother's milk. After three months, they switch to a blood meal.

Vampire bats always go for the full meal deal. They drink about half their body weight in blood each night. That sounds like a lot, but adult vampire bats only weigh about 1.5 ounces (43 grams).

Once a vampire bat finds its prey, it slices neatly into the victim with its sharp teeth. The bat then laps up the flowing red liquid like a dog at a water bowl.

The blood from most cuts **clots** quickly. How do vampire bats keep the blood flowing? They have a powerful substance in their saliva that keeps the blood from clotting.

clot—to become thicker and more solid

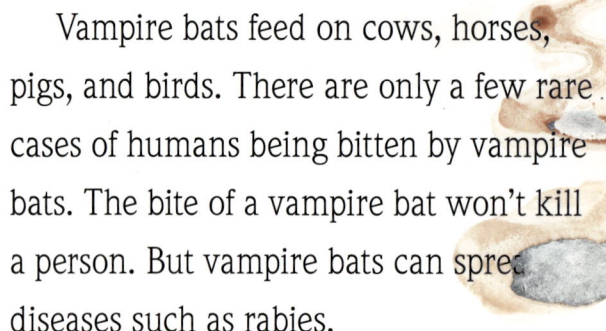

Vampire bats feed on cows, horses, pigs, and birds. There are only a few rare cases of humans being bitten by vampire bats. The bite of a vampire bat won't kill a person. But vampire bats can spread diseases such as rabies.

A Batty Name

Count Dracula famously changed into a bat in the novel Dracula. So which came first—the vampire or the vampire bat? In the 1500s, European explorers named the bats after the vampires from legend. Author Bram Stoker read about these bloodsucking bats while writing his book. He then gave Dracula the power to change into these creatures of the night.

FACT: Vampire bats pee while they eat. Peeing makes their bodies lighter. They are able to eat more and fly away more easily.

Chapter 3

Beyond Batty

It may be easy to believe vampire bats exist. But what about vampire birds? Vampire fish? Bloodsucking bugs? They're all real.

Vampire Birds

Off the coast of Ecuador lies a cluster of islands called the Galapagos Islands. These islands are home to 13 species of finches. Most of these birds prefer to feast on seeds, bugs, and nectar. But the sharp-beaked ground finch also pecks at the bodies of other birds. These "vampire birds" then slurp up tiny drops of blood.

sharp-beaked ground finch

Fishy Tales of Terror

Candiru catfish live in the Amazon River. These fish range from 1 to 6 inches (2.5 to 15 cm) long. These tiny terrors also go by the scary nickname of "vampire fish." The candiru enters the gills of larger fish and anchors itself using a spine on its head. It then hangs around for a couple of minutes to suck the other fish's blood.

candiru catfish

lamprey

lamprey teeth

Vampire fish aren't the only bloodthirsty creatures lurking in the water. Lampreys are eel-like fish ranging from 6 to 40 inches (15 to 102 cm) long. Like a shark, a lamprey's skeleton is made of **cartilage** instead of bone. But lampreys are far from spineless. Using rows of hornlike teeth, they drill deep into the flesh of other fish and suck their blood. Lampreys can be found in oceans and freshwater lakes and rivers around the world.

cartilage—strong, rubbery body tissue

A Leechy Lunch

Leeches are bloodsuckers that look like fat worms. They feed on fish, birds, frogs, and sometimes even people. Most leeches grow to no more than 8 inches (20 cm) long. The longest species, the Amazon leech, can grow up to 18 inches (46 cm) long. It pokes a 6-inch (15-cm) long **proboscis** into its victim. It then sucks up the red stuff. Leeches can be found everywhere from freshwater streams and lakes to tropical rain forests.

leech

proboscis—a long, tube-shaped mouthpart

Letting the Blood Out

For thousands of years, doctors sliced open their patients' veins to cure illnesses. This practice was called bloodletting. Doctors believed removing some blood would help balance the body's fluids. They thought that if the fluids were in balance, the patients would heal. Doctors used bloodletting to cure headaches, fevers, and broken bones. They even attached leeches to help rid patients of "bad" blood. Unfortunately, removing blood from sick people usually made them sicker. Some even died.

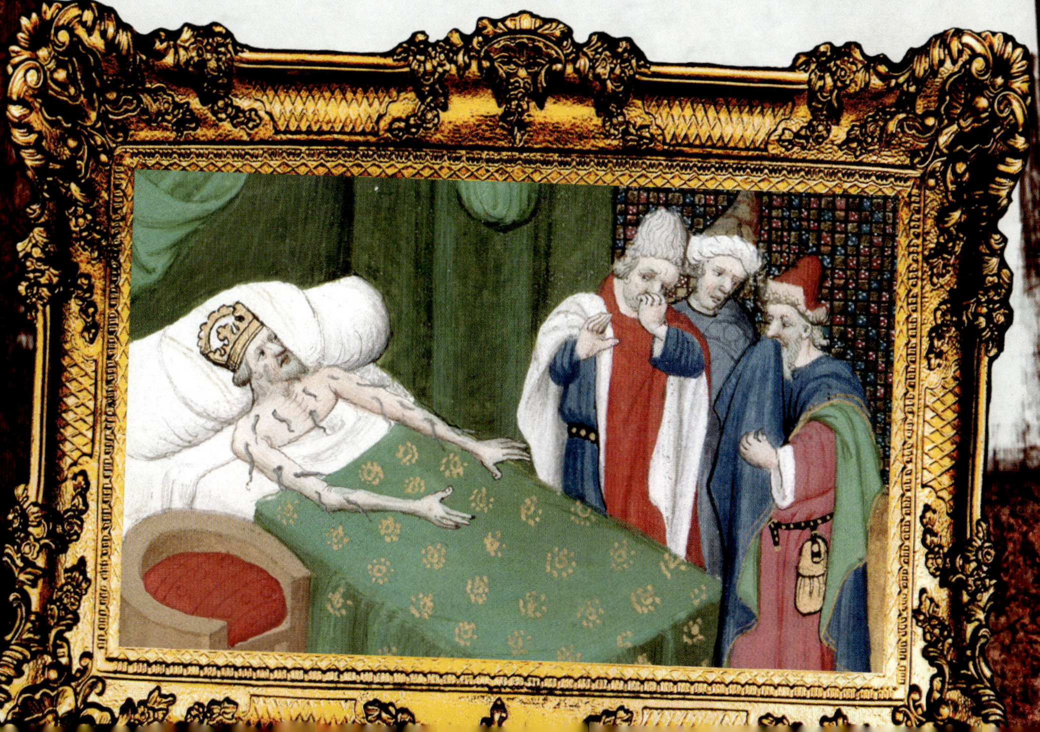

Bugging You for Blood

From ticks to mosquitoes, bloodthirsty bugs are just as creepy as all those vampire stories. Don't let their small size fool you.

More closely related to spiders than insects, ticks are eight-legged **parasites** that suck blood. There are more than 800 kinds of ticks in the world, and not one of them is up to any good.

wood tick

deer tick

parasite—an animal that needs to live on or inside another animal to survive

Ticks can't jump or fly. Instead, they crawl up tall grasses and bushes and wait for a person or animal to walk close by. Once on board, ticks chew away at the skin. They hang out for a day or more, sucking blood.

Countess Dracula

When it comes to mosquitoes, watch out for the ladies. Only female mosquitoes suck blood. They need the blood when laying eggs. Males drink nectar from flowers. Female mosquitoes land on their prey and poke the skin with a proboscis to draw blood. As a thank you for the blood meal, they may leave behind itchy, red bumps.

mosquito

Kissing Bugs

Count Dracula gave the kiss of death in the fictional tale. His kiss turned his victims into the living dead. But this bug's "kiss" just leaves the skin red and itchy. The kissing bug bites human lips, eyelids, or ears and sucks blood. It also attacks animals and other insects. About 0.5 inch (1.3 cm) long, this dark-colored bug is a living vampire.

kissing bug

Bedbugs

Like most other vampires in nature, bedbugs strike while their victims sleep. These red-brown bugs bite sleeping people and animals at night. They leave an itchy red calling card to let you know they've sucked your blood.

Bedbugs don't fly. Instead, they hitchhike or crawl from one place to another. During the day, they hide out in dark places like bird nests and bat roosts. They sometimes even hide in mattresses!

FACT: Adult bedbugs can be as large as a flat apple seed. The babies are as small as a speck of dust.

bedbug

A Scary Bite

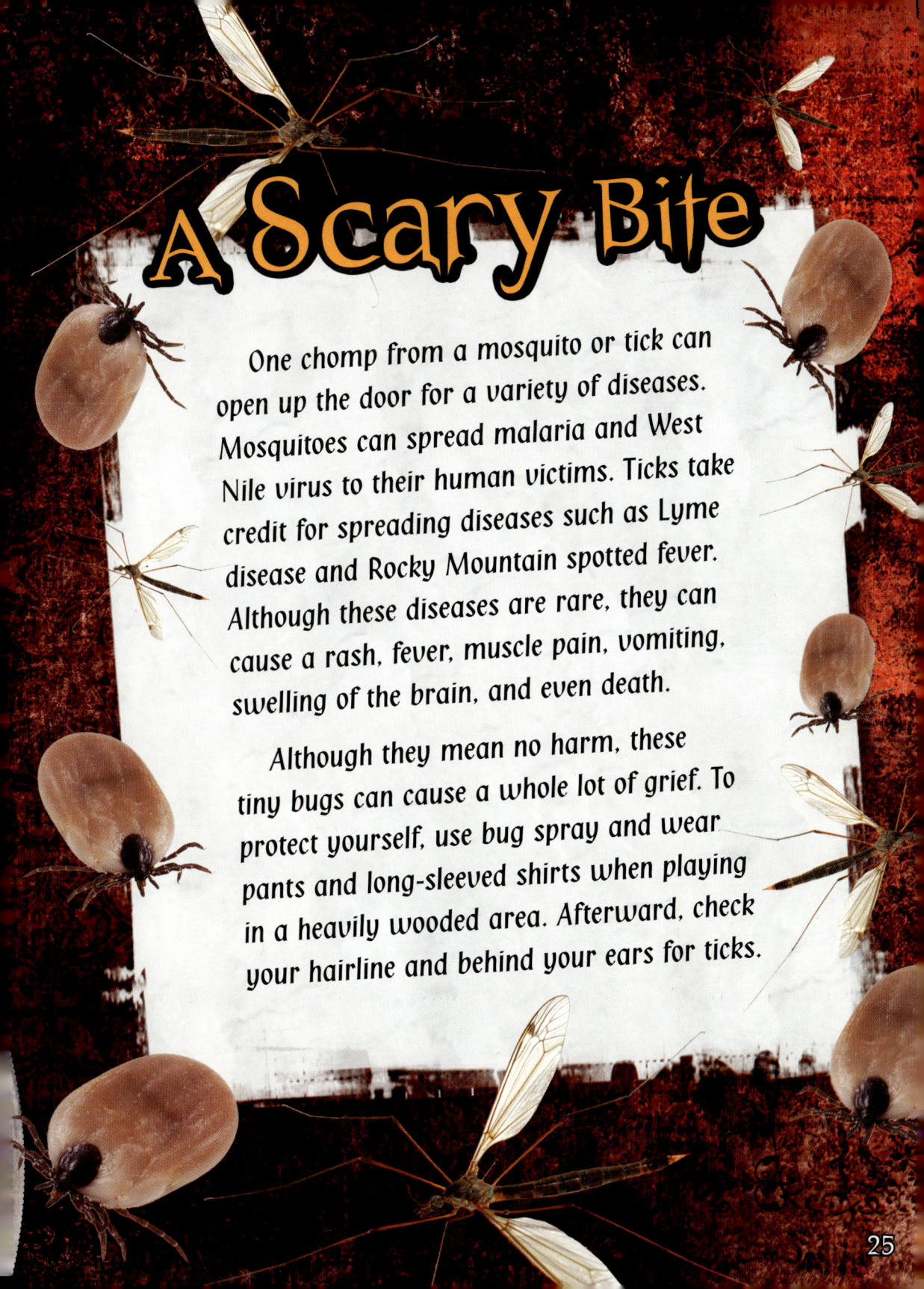

One chomp from a mosquito or tick can open up the door for a variety of diseases. Mosquitoes can spread malaria and West Nile virus to their human victims. Ticks take credit for spreading diseases such as Lyme disease and Rocky Mountain spotted fever. Although these diseases are rare, they can cause a rash, fever, muscle pain, vomiting, swelling of the brain, and even death.

Although they mean no harm, these tiny bugs can cause a whole lot of grief. To protect yourself, use bug spray and wear pants and long-sleeved shirts when playing in a heavily wooded area. Afterward, check your hairline and behind your ears for ticks.

Chapter 4
A Natural Truth

The idea of bloodsuckers in nature is really not so strange. From bats to insects, animals have much in common with legendary vampires.

The Real Bloodsuckers

Nature's vampires have existed much longer than the vampires of legend. Count Dracula's dark wardrobe is nothing new. Bats and bugs have been "wearing" black for millions of years. Fictional vampires need blood to live. Some bats, birds, fish, and insects also need blood to survive. In movies, a vampire often pierces the throat of its victim. Mosquitoes bite exposed skin, which often includes the throat, legs, arms, hands, or feet.

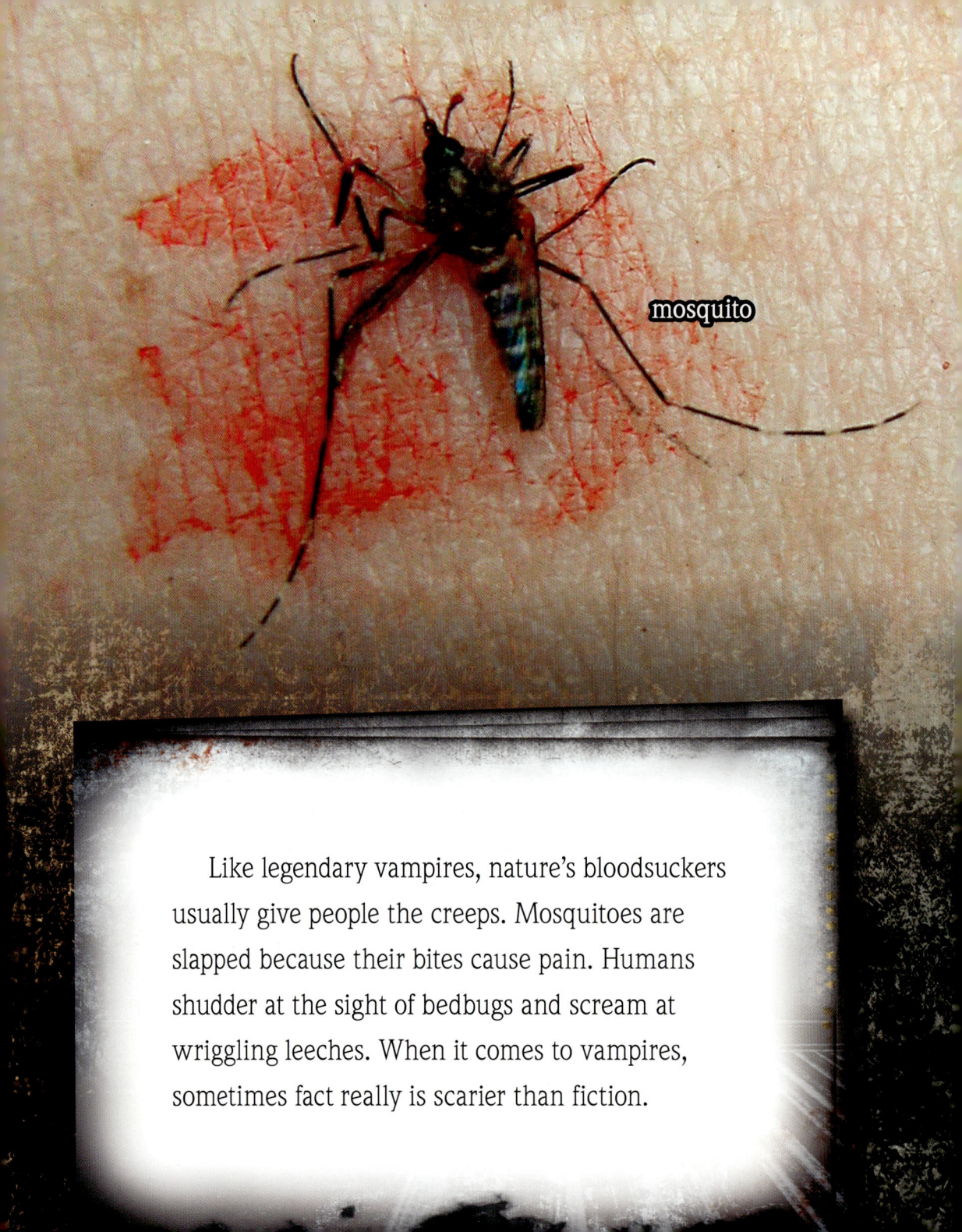

mosquito

Like legendary vampires, nature's bloodsuckers usually give people the creeps. Mosquitoes are slapped because their bites cause pain. Humans shudder at the sight of bedbugs and scream at wriggling leeches. When it comes to vampires, sometimes fact really is scarier than fiction.

Fact or Fiction?

The chupacabra is a sharp-toothed, bloodsucking creature of legend. Since the 1990s, people have reported sightings in parts of the United States, Mexico, Brazil, Chile, and Puerto Rico. People claim that this creature has fangs, big eyes, and sharp spines running down its back. This secretive monster has been blamed for draining the blood of livestock. But like the Loch Ness Monster and Bigfoot, chupacabras might not exist. Scientists have yet to find any.

FACT: Chupacabra means "goatsucker" in Spanish.

Glossary

cartilage (KAHR-tuh-lij)—the strong, rubbery body tissue that makes up the skeletons of some fish

clot (KLOT)—to become thicker and more solid

insect (IN-sekt)—a small animal with a hard outer shell, six legs, three body sections, and two antennae; most insects have wings

nocturnal (nok-TUR-nuhl)—active at night; nocturnal animals rest during the day

parasite (PAIR-uh-site)—an animal or plant that needs to live on or inside another animal or plant to survive

prey (PRAY)—an animal hunted by another animal for food

proboscis (pro-BOS-kiss)—a long, tube-shaped mouthpart that some animals use to drink liquid

rabies (RAY-beez)—a deadly disease that people and animals can get from the bite of an infected animal

roost (ROOST)—a place where a bat sleeps and rests

species (SPEE-sheez)—a group of animals or plants that shares common characteristics

Read More

Landau, Elaine. *Bats: Hunters of the Night.* Animals After Dark. Berkeley Heights, N.J.: Enslow Publishers, 2008.

Marx, Mandy R. *Great Vampire Legends.* Vampires. Mankato, Minn.: Capstone Press, 2011.

Neuman, Pearl. *Bloodsucking Leeches.* No Backbone! The World of Invertebrates. New York: Bearport Pub., 2009.

Somervill, Barbara A. *Ticks: Digging for Blood.* Bloodsuckers. New York: PowerKids Press, 2008.

Internet Sites

FactHound offers a safe, fun way to find Internet sites related to this book. All of the sites on FactHound have been researched by our staff.

Here's all you do:

Visit *www.facthound.com*

FactHound will fetch the best sites for you!

INDEX

bedbugs, 24, 28

bloodletting, 19

candiru catfish, 16, 17

chupacabra, 29

Count Dracula, 4, 6, 12, 23, 26

diseases, 12, 25
    protection against, 25

Dracula (novel), 6, 7, 12

kissing bugs, 23

lampreys, 17

leeches, 18, 19, 28

mosquitoes, 20, 22, 25, 26, 28

sharp-beaked ground finches, 15

Stoker, Bram, 7, 12

ticks, 20–21, 25

vampire bats, 4, 8, 9, 10, 12, 13, 14, 26

Vlad Dracula, 7